# FAMOUS SALLY

*Shirley Jackson*

# Famous
# Sally

*Pictures by Chas. B. Slackman*

*A Harlin Quist Book*

Published by Harlin Quist, Incorporated
Distributed by Crown Publishers, Incorporated

Library of Congress Catalog Card Number: AC 66-10753
Copyright © Harlin Quist, Incorporated 1966
All rights reserved
First Printing • Printed in the United States of America

Designed by John Bradford

No one in the world had ever heard of Sally. No one in the world knew Sally's name. No one ever said to her, "Good morning, Sally," or "Where are you going today, Sally?" or "What a pretty blue dress you are wearing, Sally" —if, of course, she should happen to be wearing a pretty blue dress at the time.

"I wish everyone knew my name," Sally said. "I wish I could hear everyone saying Sally Sally Sally."

She washed her face and hands and put on a blue dress—in case anyone should want to tell her it was pretty—and then she said, "I will make people say my name. I am Sally and I will make the people in all the cities say my name."

The first city she picked was Tall City. The buildings in Tall City were so high they wore clouds on their heads like hats. The people in Tall City walked on stilts because the doorways were so high, and the children hung their swings from the very tops of the trees.

"I must have my name very high for Tall City," Sally said. "What is the highest thing I know? A kite." So Sally made a kite out of white paper. The kite was ten miles and three feet wide and eleven miles and six inches long. On it Sally wrote S A L L Y in black paint. She tied thirty-one miles of string on her kite and took it into the yard behind her house.

Then she tossed the kite into the air and the wind caught it and up it sailed, higher and higher and higher, right through the clouds and across the sky until it sailed over the tall tops of the buildings in Tall City.

SALLY said the kite over Tall City, and the people in the streets of Tall City looked up and looked up and looked up.

"Sally," they said to each other, "that kite says Sally. Sally," they said, "Sally Sally."

"Now the people in Tall City know my name," Sally said.

The next city was Small City. The buildings in Small City were so low that people could sit down on their roofs and drink tea from a cup on the chimney. When the people in Small City went visiting each other they stepped in through the second-story windows, and once a cat chasing a mouse jumped right over a house.

"I must have a very small name for Small City," Sally said. "What is the smallest thing I know? My little walking doll is the smallest thing I know." So Sally put her little walking doll in a box and went to the very edge of Small City. She took her little walking doll out of the box and put her on the ground and wound her walker and her talker and started the little walking doll down the streets of Small City.

Sallysallysallysallysallysallysallysallysallysallysallysallysallysallysallysallysallysallysallysallysallysallysallysallysallysallysallysa

"Sallysallysallysallysally," said the little walking doll, walking one foot after the other down the streets of Small City. "Sallysally."

The people on the street in Small City looked down at the little walking doll, and the people drinking tea on the roofs of Small City looked down on the little walking doll walking one foot after

sally

another down the street saying "Sally-
sallysally."

"Sally," said the people of Small
City to each other. "That little walking
doll is saying Sally. Sally," they said.
"Sallysally."

"Now the people in Small City know
my name," Sally said.

The third city was Soft City. Everyone in Soft City was so quiet that the
babies sang lullabies to themselves and
all the people wore shoes made of cat fur
so their feet would not make a sound on
the streets. Their houses were made of
pillows and they wore marshmallows for
hats.

"I must have a very soft name for Soft City," Sally said. "What is the softest thing I know? The wind is the softest thing I know." So she went into her backyard and called the wind. "Please, please come," she called softly, "please, wind, come." The wind came and wound around and around Sally, whispering in her ear and tickling her hair. "Will you tell the people of Soft City my name?" Sally asked the wind, and the wind turned a little circle in Sally's hair and lifted a leaf off the ground and made a laughing noise in a buttercup and floated away to Soft City.

"Sallyallyallyallyally," the wind sang in the streets of Soft City. "Sally-allyally," and the people in Soft City turned their soft faces under the marsh-mallow hats and listened to the wind.

"Sally," they said to each other. "Listen to the wind; it is saying Sally. Sally," they said, "Sally."

"Now the people in Soft City know my name," Sally said.

The next city was Rose City. In Rose City the people planted roses in their gardens and in their houses and in the parks, and all the buildings had roses growing along their tops. There were roses growing in a row down the middle of the street. There were roses in window boxes, and all the people wore roses in their buttonholes and in their hair.

"What will take my name to Rose City?" Sally said. "What do roses love best? Honeybees," she said. "I will ask the honeybees to tell my name to the people of Rose City."

Sally went to the queen bee and the queen bee said, "Of course. My bees and I love to visit Rose City, and we will gladly tell the people there your name."

So the queen bee and nine thousand and eleven other bees flew in a great bee cloud to Rose City. They landed on the roses in the streets and the gardens and the people's heads.

"Zzzzzally," the bees sang loudly,

"zzzzzally, zzzzzally, zzzzzally," and the people laughed because the bees were on all their roses.

"Sally," the people said, laughing, "listen to the bees saying Sally. Sally," they said, "Sally."

"Now the people in Rose City know my name," Sally said.

The next city was Play City. In Play City every day was a holiday all year round. The people dressed up like pirates or clowns or black cats, and they played leapfrog and jumprope and hide-and-go-seek all day long. In Play City every day was someone's birthday and every day they had a birthday party.

"What will take my name to Play City?" Sally said. "What is the happiest thing I know? A merry-go-round. I will send a merry-go-round to Play City to tell the people there my name." Sally went to the park where the merry-go-round was resting between rides and said, "Please, dear merry-go-round, will you carry my name to Play City?"

"Play City sounds like a fine place," the merry-go-round said, "I would be happy to carry your name there."

So the merry-go-round wheeled along beside Sally to the edge of Play City and then the merry-go-round began to go round and round and round, up and down the streets of Play City.

"Sally-go-round," sang the merry-go-round, "Sally-go-round, Sally-go-round, Sally-go-round." And the people of Play City stopped their games of ball and leapfrog and came to the merry-go-round to ask for a ride.

"Sally-go-round," sang the merry-

go-round, and the people said to each other, "Do you hear what the merry-go-round is saying? It is saying Sally. Sally," they said, "Sally."

"And now Play City knows my name," Sally said.

The next city was Slow City. Here the people moved like water dripping from a faucet. Step, they went. Step. Step. Step. When the people of Slow City ate their breakfasts they ate so slowly

that when they were through it was time for lunch, and when one Slow City person said to another, "Good morning, how are you?" it took an hour and twenty minutes.

"What will take my name to Slow City?" Sally said. "How can I make the people of Slow City know my name? What is the slowest thing I know? A turtle."

So Sally asked a turtle friend of hers
if he would take her name to Slow City
and the turtle thought for a long time,
because turtles take a long time to do
anything, and then the turtle said in his
careful voice, "Of course I will take your
name to Slow City, Sally. I would like
to visit there, anyway." Sally painted
her name S A L L Y in bright red on the
turtle's back, and because she could not
wait for the turtle to walk to Slow City
she put him in her wagon and pulled him
to the edge of Slow City and then set him
down on the street.

Down the street the turtle went, with his back saying S A L L Y. He looked carefully at everything he passed, turning his head from one side to the other, and the people of Slow City turned very slowly to look at him.

"Why is that turtle going so fast?" they asked each other, "why is he in such a hurry? He says Sally on his back," they said, "look, that fast turtle says Sally on his back. Sally," they said, "Sally."

"And now the people of Slow City know my name," Sally said.

The last city was Noisy City. In Noisy City all the people and the dogs and the cats and the birds made noise. They ran shouting through the streets and they slammed doors and they threw pots and pans out of upstairs windows to hear them crash in the street. All the people in Noisy City carried firecrackers in their pockets and set them off all day long. There were thirty-seven brass bands in Noisy City and they played all day long, and eleven times a day the fire sirens blew just for fun.

"What will take my name to Noisy City?" Sally said. "What is loudest thing I know? A drum." So Sally got a big big drum seven feet across and she brought it to the edge of Noisy City and started down the street banging and banging on the drum.

"Sally boom boom," the drum roared, "Sally boom boom Sally boom boom Sally boom boom." But no one in Noisy City heard the drum at all. The people were making too much noise with the firecrackers and the brass bands and the pots and pans crashing on the sidewalk. Sally went from one end of Noisy City to the other, with the drum roaring "Sally boom boom Sally boom boom," and no one heard her at all.

"What shall I do?" Sally said, "What shall I do? I must make the people of Noisy City know my name. I know what I will do."

She set the drum on the edge of
Noisy City and ran home quickly. Then
she brought everything to Noisy City.
She brought the bees and the wind and
the little walking doll and the turtle and
the merry-go-round and the kite. She
brought them all.

The kite sailed high in the air over Noisy City, saying S A L L Y in big black letters, and the bees sang "Zzzzally zzzzally zzzzally," and the little walking doll walked down the street putting one foot after the other and saying "Sally-sallysally," and the wind sang softly "Sallyallyally Sallyallyally Sallyally-ally," and the turtle walked along looking from one side to the other in his careful way, and on his back it said S A L L Y in red letters, and the merry-go-round sang "Sally-go-round Sally-go-round Sally-go-round," and the big bass drum roared "Sally boom boom Sally boom boom Sally boom boom," and S A L L Y they all went, "go round boom boom."

Then the people of Noisy City began to look around and they said to each other, "Sally. Look at the turtle and the kite. Listen to the wind. Listen to the drum. Look at the bees. Sally," they said, "Sally, Sally, Sally."

And now all the world had heard of
Sally. Everyone knew her name. People
came up to her and said, "Good morning,
Sally," and "Where are you going today,
Sally?" and "What a pretty blue dress
you are wearing, Sally"—if, of course,
she should happen to be wearing a pretty
blue dress at the time.

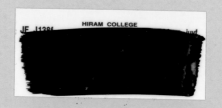